Gone Away

To Coral Dreams
In the Ocean of Air

By
Band of Brothers

Edited by
M. H. Wolf

Dedication

To *Mark Wittbecker*, our brother, who was interested in biology and cryogenics, who liked to play baseball, who was always laughing, and who is always with us.

Gone Away

To Coral Dreams in the Ocean of Air
Under the Darkness Between Stars
Where Eidolons are Invisible
With the Ecstasy
of Hiding

By
Band of Brothers

Edited By
Morgan Hood Wolf

Calliope Press
2006

Acknowledgments
International Publications, 1976, for "Resumption of Innocence."
Palouse, 1981 "Ecstasy of Weeds"
Writer's Digest, 1983, for "Memory."
World of Poetry, 1983, for "Eidolon Lost."
Wind Row, 1983, for "Three Nights in the Heart of the Earth"
Night Wolves for "Wolf Loves to Hide" "Lightbearer"
Wild Apples for "Knowing Why" "Forest Passage"
A.M. Caratheodory for "Dragon" (cover art)
       and "Snakeman" (backcover art)h

This Calliope Press Edition of *Gone Away*
is Published by Band of Brothers Productions
for Three Muses Books, M&RW, Ltd.

Published in the United States
by Mozart & Reason Wolfe, Ltd., Wilmington
Prepared and produced by
Calliope Press, Boston
Designed by Rian Garcia Calusa, Tallevast

Please address all correspondence for
M&RW, Ltd., Calliope Press,
and Band of Brothers,
to: editor@3musesbooks.com

Publisher's Cataloging in Publication Data

Band of Brothers 1946 1948 1950

  Gone Away

ISBN 0-911385-30-4

Printed in the United States of America

Contents

The Act

Fragments Found
Oh
Thousands and thousands of flowers in bloom
and none can dispel my enveloping gloom,
hundreds and hundreds of flowers to wear
and none ever grace my embracing stone tomb.
No
the flowers that I walk among
can never lift my lowly spirit;
though they are fresh and life
is young—still, I want to end it
When
soon all the flowers will die
and visit me where I will lie
and though so different in name
the dust will feel just the same.
Yes
Death is a welcome path
for feet that traveled far
and for a mind too tired
escape to a hidden star
Then
these eyes won't see the dawn
where love lies heavy now
and living less and less—
the glory of living is gone
So
bitterly I shoved
a bullet hard inside—
I lived unloving and unloved
and thus I will have died.

No Alternative

Someone is gone
who couldn't have lived with love.
There should be a stone around
to mark the body in the ground,
there should be a door
some boundary to mark the passing.
There should be more
than just my tired memory.

"There was so much that I did not receive
all quietly offered all that I could have
but would not take and being so unanchored
drifted into death."

Someone is missing who said he couldn't live
without love. There should be something
that you could have done to make his act less foolish—
feeling just a little sad and when you're lying alone
maybe renewing a few tears.

"I want no more of misery, no more refusals
to suffocate desire. I don't like trying,
I don't like failing, maybe I can make
a poem of dying."

But, what would I say if I could think of words?
If I would want to leave them for you
I would not want to go.

"But you will find me and be left at last wondering,
maybe find the verse left on paper by someone else
who went before me. There was one alternative
to love, there was no alternative for me, but
I do not trifle before need, I do not vacillate
on logic's answer."

Lament of the Universal King

They tell of planets trembling when my vision dims
one ray. They say the stars will disappear without
my willing sight. They tell of oceans ending when
my breathing last expires. They say the sea will turn
to dust to mourn my final breath.
They tell of daystar darkening when my heartbeats fade
away. They say the sun will cease to shine without
my life to light. They tell of heaven trembling when
my restless soul retires. They say the sky will sink
to earth to mourn my carnal death.
They speak of earthly fires. They prophecy that crashing
galaxies will herald the end of all. They speak
of universal death.

Weep for Me

Look at me, look at me.
Look at what I am,
quick before I die—
get a record in your memory
put my picture down on film
mark my words, list my deeds
and get it all arranged,
quick, before I die.

Think of me who never loved
Think of me and cry
Weep for me whom no one loved,
weep for me, I die.

The Aftermath

Funeral

One body in a grave
is someone's fifty dollars
and a soul with blessings for the lord.
That body was your name
and passed away like money,
freshly minted, spent that day;
pictures start to fade,
thoughts replace your laughter
and tears are salt sprays dropping towards
the plastic flowers on
the stone above your coffin.
Could I have been closer, I ask,
who really didn't know you so well, after all?

Accuse

Mark is dead! Let him lie
for he was one who chose to die,
one who thought of life too little
or weighed his thought too much,
who lingered barely out of touch
until being hopelessly driven
to one irrational impulse given.

Now is too late to offer your aid
unless you wish to try and save
the life of another caught the same
in stinking webs of your opinion—
you, uncaring, are to blame!

Broken

—broken kitten by the roadside
trembled once and died—
when I came the blood had dried,
the body was cold, a black and white
bundle of fur so soft and light
and light in years I imagined him yet
as being alive,
wanting to play
but always his way
and never yours, making a game
of climbing a tree, never the same,
finding a path, preparing for
adventures to be tried
or trying to run far
from something denied,
on a new course
with little remorse,
struck by a car
and tossed unnoticed aside—
who couldn't see,
the road was so wide?

Someone had loved him,
given him a name,
was missing him, feeling blame
but what to me
but someone's pride
and thing of beauty,
bound by love, unbound by any duty—
I covered him with dirt
and leaves of gold
silently sighed,
and I and someone somewhere cried.

The Sun

The sun has died, the sun is buried deep.
The earth is dark, no light will ever light
the darkness left behind.
He walked into the forest of the night
never to return.

That eyeless depth with promise of a sleep
that all men try to find
may just contain a heavy earthen bed
and wise men might discern
that conscious life relies on conscious sight
and none are made as blind
as those who walk that darkling wood of fright—
remember brightness, the sun is dead!

Nothing Said

Flesh is so tentative
that others mourn its release he thought
Black birds with black wings
flocked over dried blood as he watched.
The oak dropped old leaves
over dry brown grass— he listened
One woman comforted another
in front of the window; he felt.
Walking outside he flies
with the birds of ease and emptiness
nowhere
And there he dwells
there light is born there in stillness.
Memory of birds standing
over time he unfolds being.
Wind ruffles feathers, the birds look,
flying, as leaves turn red and drop there.

What of Her (Passing Years)

Two passing years
beyond all expressing
all cure and redressing
the void seems as vast
and tears run as fast
as ever before.

And after those years
your heart more acutely
more madly and mutely
cries futilely after
him and his laughter
to fill in the core.

In spite of those years
the wound has not mended
diminished or blended
the ache is as vast
and tears race as fast
as ever before.

Regardless of years
and time spent hoping
the end of your groping
will find him thereafter
when you hear his laughter
and see him once more.

Patterns

The flame that made the pattern died
but the pattern resides
in other patterns now and can be
transmitted abstractly.
The matter that held the pattern
has been returned to its source,
but the pattern has been impressed
onto other patterns, concretely.
Divided, diluted, unrecognizable,
except in resurrections in accidental lyrics
or strange and mythic dreams,
where time progresses
when it hasn't, along alternate
lines, with altered facts.

You, I am host for patterns remaining
without flames or flesh, patterns depending
on my burning and turning in ascending
spirals to burst in an ecstasy of multiple
eyes in an invisible night—ideal topological
impassioned neural lives are lived in me
as real possibilities.
Let the patterns miniaturized in the whole
hearted world expand to nebulae—
white apple flesh beneath the yellow skin
unlimited by gravity, or by colors
we have seen. It is possible.
                    Be.

Con Morituis

I see him running in my memory
around the house, squirt gun loaded
and ready for battle.
I see him frowning in my memory
over the darkness between stars—
Why study light, he asked,
there's so little to mold its brother, night?
I see him searching in my memory
for life in its beginning,
the archegonium beneath the lens
is silent; our breathing is the flower
that cannot find its origin.
I cannot see him at all now, perhaps
I cannot wake, or waking will be
him, finally mourning me.

Mark at 20

I wondered what you would look like now
then I look in the mirror and see how
we look alike. I gained weight, you lost
some. Your smile is mine now, although
I rarely use it for anything but night.

Mark at 31

Where was I this year when I thought of you?
I was following wolves at night, looking through
a green Russian night scope, trying to tell
them apart from pigs or deer. I lay
on the cold ground and slept
for a while, wondering if you could be seen
in a certain kind of light, running
through some distant green landscape.

Mark at 42

Every year, around the equinox that measures
the length of light and measures the depth of my loss
a thought slowly opens in me
that Mark died on this day.
So every year I stop and think
knowing that he can not—I remember
where he is and remember where I was that day
And this year I was in a mountain
wilderness lying on yellow grasses
watching clouds reform like fantasies
in water, feeling the mist fall on my face
and wondering how much higher
I could climb before the light faded
and determined where I had to rest,
and I think to him:
                              You could be here with me,
if you had not thought
that an moment's romantic impulse
was more important than lying together, brothers
just the two of us, like beasts
beneath the sun and rain on a bed
of mosses and grasses—having collected
all the intervening days of listening
to other voices with other messages, other
attractions, distractions, and dreams,
and then conversing about them.

No one misses you like your brother
but I am only that and I was not there
to countermand your decision to die
the one that should have been mine
and I only wait now, and you wait I know,
but I no longer hurry, for time is not mine
any longer; in the depth and chaos of the flow
I am only an eddy, collecting
experiences for both of us
a few thoughts and a few words
that I cannot rehearse
with anyone else.

Mark at 53

You think that it's over, but it isn't.
It never ends, it just unravels
until the threads become thinner and break,
until they become dimmer
and you lose sight of them.
But, we could trace them all
and reweave part of the pattern
until we are together in some way
not the same, but not totally lost
or completely alone either.
We are together in imagination
and dreams, in memories woven
in different patterns, not as rich
and not as present as the past,
but still present as part of us.

Mark at 64

This year, just before your birthday,
I learned that I had a terminal
incurable cancer of the blood. Strange
to hear how one will probably die,
especially when there is plenty of time, a year
or two. enough time to make closure,
to explain or to say goodbye
but never enough to do all the living
expected for twenty more years—Still,
I expect life to stretch to fill
the new horizon as the moments
stretched to fill the entire last turn
of your life.

Mark at 100

I have seen my father's grief, and grandmother's,
for you, the distant son and brother,
like any human grief, limited by
the expression of muscles or words, filtered
by time and distance,
and the shift of memories
and the evolution of emotion
and I have continued their line
and as the words live you may feel
a little of the rage or resignation,
at the act of autothanatosis,
or compliance and acceptance
of the flow that carries us
and then disperses us in the end
until the particles are elsewhere
and the patterns blur
and the images change
until there are only words
and their meanings have changed
and it seems like a play
or comedy of manners
long ago.

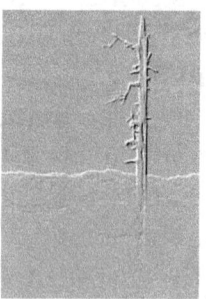

The view from the tree

The Life

Hamadryad

Hundred-seventy feet high with blue-green needles,
obtuse with small bracts and blue-purple cones—
the tree is so unexpected from the seed.
My day off: I wanted to try to climb this clean
and dry old pine, set off from the rest.
I jumped up to a low dead limb and pulled myself up,
exultant. I touched and felt
the roughness of the bark, felt the trunk sway
and roots strain with a delicate breeze. I went
up further and looked out across the hills, carefully
not thinking of death or pain or nothingness.

This measured thing is mostly space confounded
by small unpredictabilities, opaque, as impenetrable
to my eyes as to my hands and feet. Emptier now that
the dryads have deserted. I clung securely, moved slowly
higher some hills and valleys shades of brown
and violet-shaded—I saw my body below, shattered
on the needle floor. The branches seemed more treacherous
but I reached the height of a near-by tree, saw
distant mountains and plains. The branches are younger
and firmer but much closer together. I squirmed
through the highest ones, freshened by the wind,
but worried by it all the same. I reached to top—now
I have her height, but she has my mind.
Just to my left, a blasted snag, relict of a moment
when fingers of wood and fingers of lightning met,
and white fire exchanged its life for the life of a pine
leaving mute wood and a black spine.
Swaying, feel the rhythm of respiration lift branches
spread to collect light and cool air around the trunk,
push downwards into the earth to hold and reach out
for minerals and waters—a double life of light and dark,
inside out, a cone of slow fire drawing air, water,

the fire of life drawing earth upwards.

I watched clouds and hawks, as I slowed my breathing
to match her pace. So slow, so long . . .
Later, I tore off a small branch, hurried down,
rubbing bark and skin, heart struggling
with having gotten too close to something unknown,
jumped the last ten feet to the ground, groaning, sighing,
smiling, prize in hand, wearing a crown of needles and lichen,
wondering what kind of change—
She is not solid—there is so much room for spirits
to pass through, unhurried, or perhaps stay. Again
I looked back at transplanted hearts passing
through trees leaving molecular shadows in amber;
the hamadryad has not left, and I am hers.

(The Greek dryads were conceived by earth [Gaea] from
the blood of heaven [Uranus], castrated by his son,
Time [Chronos], for refusing to let his bothers Briareus
and Cottus into the light. These nymphs, beautiful females
of divine origin, were given the guardianship of the woods
and the trees. Wood-nymphs were Dryads, tree-nymphs
were Hamadryads, Fruit-tree-nymphs were Meliades,
and other nymphs haunted mountains, valleys,
and meadows. The Dryads, who lived in groves
were free to move about, in trees and out. They often
associated with Artemis, goddess of the hunt.
The Hamadryads, who dwelled in individual trees,
died with their trees— each tree cries in anguish when cut).

Prayer for All Dead Beings (A Secret Place)

The eyes burst before
seeing; the ruptured bag leaked
fluids that no longer nourished
muscles that could not move.
Gravel-crusted fur is outrageous and displaced
on blacktop, suffering a variety of stares
from the aliens, whose trivial
concerns blotted out any awareness.
May hands as unknown as those that struck
you down carry you to a hidden place
in weeds and there return you
to the earth in secret.
All beings need a private death, a private
place to turn at last and lie still.

(Racer was my friend, a skunk who came home
with my cat Hank-Ra every day to eat buttered
toast on the grass in front of the window)

Colors

It is most important for you to see
what I am being
not what I have achieved,
what I have seen not what I have received.
Look who I've experienced
impressive in themselves; look at what
I've shared not evaluated or compared.
You stated all your goals
and set out to attain them, you reduced
the entire spectrum to one solitary ray
and measured different colors by it—
all my colors with your grey.

Of the Same Flesh

Am I not the arm you grew
to reach out to others to help
the crippled who could
not climb as high as you?
Am I not the leg you made
to step wherever it could
to people sleeping in streets
who cannot travel to be paid?
Are my eyes not to see
the sum of human misery
and this mind not know
and this heart not feel?
Will you grow apart now
that I've done these things
awkwardly, wastefully,
but open and well-meaning?
Are we not still the same in body,
mind and name?
Or does that knowledge hurt
and you cannot look?

Leaving Port

Oh, Dad, my dearest love,
you carried yourself in silence.
But, you know you can't be hurt
that I'm not just like you
when all your effort meant
to make me different
(I would have been so happy
in your place, with your life,
having your job's fulfillment,
your contentment, your wife).
You know I owe you this much:
to do the things you haven't done.
Your life has been my port and platform
and if my ship seems lost at sea
or floats directionless in space
your life has been my dock
you were there for me to leave,
you gave me the need to know
and so I had no choice but go.
Don't worry that I'm lost now
that no one charted a course
or left markers here before,
I'll make my way somehow.

Inheritance

Our fathers all were poor
poorer far than we are
but richer, so much richer
than their own before.
What riches have you
that make me poor without,
what dear things give security
that I would be mad to doubt?
Do questions turn your head
does suffering make you pure?
Do you know what was said,
will you have faith anyway
and wait until you're dead?
Have you tried going without,
have you ever given thought
to no greed or hunger ever,
to sharing all that we have—
no abstract loyalty to flags
countries, or corporations?

The wealth of fathers accrues
by generations—it may be our trust,
but it is our wrong and sorrow, too.

Silently

You gave me special favors
and I took them as my right,
you sheltered me from problems
and kept them from my sight.
How often did you not control
me or when I was in pain, not stay?
How often did you not direct me
so I would not foolishly turn away?
How often have I thoughtlessly hurt
You because you thought it would be good
for me to go and simply desert you
because you didn't seem to be good?
But, I was wrong to judge you then
for yours was a quiet selflessness
to give me the best that you could.
Now your declining years make
me see with increasing clearness
what I could never see in our early nearness—
your dying silently for my sake.

Award for juvenile delinquency

Lost

"To explore is dangerous enough, but
to discover, you must be lost.
Distrust everything, whatever seems;
question reasons, question dreams;
leave home.
Who follows his whispering blood
and wanders in confusion, who surrenders
to confusion, wastes time searching—
He is lost.

He is lost without a goal, who watches
without desire to own, who tackles
the labyrinth without thread or help,
who grows too slowly and unfolds
uncertainly. He is lost who is too
too changeable, who goes in too many
directions and tries too many times
without calculating
the cost.

He is lost who dies, and lives and dies
again, each time as sadly, bearing
the memory of the time before, each time
with pain the heart more sensitively bore.
He is lost
who makes his own path—"

"But, where is security, and where
is the dignity in being free?"

"Is water respectable?" Yet who cannot
consider it? Are clouds not dignified?
Who can hold them?"

Joseph Transported

People die in pain, life is smashed
life is shortened, death sustained,
minds torn apart, minds compressed,
bodies poisoned, bodies fired,
bodies crushed.

The whole world stopped him
the whole world stopped then—
where was the boundary?
When eyes could not open?
His heart quieted, did it beat
again? Did it end? When?

In that moment when you touched
him, he was simple and complete—
there was no softer day, no gentler
way than quietly in sleep transported
in a caul of dreams away.

The house by the orchard

Winona Stars

Late spring and the cycle was cresting
with a fresh troupe of players
and Winona, sensing the end of her act
yet holding the stage together
gathered light behind her eyes
to express the feelings left.
Her hands composed
her eyes focused and flared then dimmed
and released their light.
We return the ashes but keep our hologram
images for memories. All her movements
were illuminated, her skin reflected light
and the caress of photons carried messages
to the stars. If we could overtake
the waves of light, we would find her standing
in her nightgown three years out, then sitting
on the porch with Joseph long past Centaurus
clowning with her children at forty years
distance, and once, beyond Arcturus, a sweet maiden
standing frozen in a garden for the first photograph—
the youth, the girl, the baby
moving outwards on expanding spheres
of light towards other galaxies. If we could somehow
wait eighty-two light years away and collect
the rays from earth in a lens of slow glass
we might see all her motions relived.
But, it would not be her. We have our memories
and we renew her through our lives.
The troupe is young, but adventurous
and accomplished; they play on a path
with blue bachelor buttons
in a mist of light. It is almost summer.

The Orchard

Over the hill a white orchard
blooms over spring shadows;
weathered house long abandoned
over a fallen porch, the dining room
window black without glass.
Light moves, so I walk closer
hugging my sides for warmth
then press my face against
a surviving pane, hooding
my eyes, hand on a surface
of nonreflecting fluid, not
drinking—then the years repeal—
pushed forward from pain-etched
shadows, my father Walter's face, wan, remote
from this green present and Bessie's, lined
from work, gazing out the new window
towards what?—the grey and shapeless
future when the house has passed to ruin
the furnishings to distant hands
and their essences reduced to photographs?—
but not with bitterness, with understanding.

The image passed, line by line:
What we create we cannot hold
but must let grow beyond.
The past closed up, the wind
stirred the cherry blossoms.

Not Caring

I liked to have my hair cut
when I was young
because I liked the feel
of it. And when I played
at games I didn't care who won,
I just enjoyed all of the movement
breaking tackles and circling around
to give everyone another chance.
I liked to ride our bike down hills
of dirt jump off at full speed
and not get hurt—maybe just
a few bruises. I hunted
the Benson's stream for little minnows
sometimes catching them in bowls
sometimes letting them go.
I had to tumble in the backyard grass
even if it meant I had to take a bath
to stop the itching so.
I stalked the forest on unexplored
trails sighting every unknown animal.
But, I don't do it anymore.
Now I just coast through the years
and the coasting isn't even fun
and I wish that I could learn a way
to see things as if I was young
again, see them for the first time
and not even care too much.

Leaves

I sprawled at ease beneath the autumn trees and watched
   the falling leaves
              as one leaf, then
                 another, frees
           its stem and leaves
        its limb and weaves
    a spiraled loop
        and starts to swoop
        and swirl,
          dip and twirl
       before so quickly sinking
    in a final helpless whirl.
And after, when the leaves unfurl and lay there linking
   I lay here thinking:
          They fell too fast
              and these at last
                will drown
          in oceans on the ground
       of leaves of yellow brown.
I bid the leaves slow down, slow down and not surround
me with the sound
      of rustled sighing,
         to stop their wayward flying
           and drop tomorrow
     if at all.
I bid the breeze continue dying and not keep trying
   to steal leaves off blazing trees
     but be at a moment's call
       to do that which I please that it will do.
I bid the leaves slow down and let me catch a few
    before the winter freeze restrains them in a mound
   in stiffened waves on still-blown seas.
I bid the hurried leaves slow down and give me time
for thinking, before the coming winter chains
them to the ground, for, when they
are bound, I am too.

Dancing

I saw you dancing by yourself
in a room half-dark with memory,
felt gravity loose its gentle bonds
and the earth slow down while you spun
wordlessly alone, almost unseen,
twirling around in a dream
flying away, you know, with me.

What music have you always carried so,
how many thousand miles ago?
Where would I look to find
the origin of that celestial motion
that keeps the footprints on the rug
two steps behind? I saw you
with your arms folded on your bosom
but ready to sweep any unwary
preoccupied man or record album
into your exciting embrace.

I saw your legs move through your skirts
I saw your hair unbound and flowing
I saw the light in your face.
How many times was this the joy's
only possible expression,
how often lifted you from depression
how often was all direction lost—
the entire world lost—
that you could discover the one within?

All the stars were spinning, and planets
and stones, falling leaves
waltzing in a whirl
turning to snowflakes in a swirl
in clouds spiraling like atom-patterns
dancing, and you, and you.

The First

No more life can overpower
that first infatuation; the world
cannot ever be harder, or clearer,
or come closer than when it arrived
there and then with you.
No subsequent love can rebuild
in the permanent vacuum
after the first infatuation died—
The world cannot be more vacant
and lonely without you.

Resumption of Innocence

Where was I before I learned of things
I wished to learn no more?
Hasn't my body renewed itself
My self forgotten the pain?
Must I be burdened by experience
or can I start forgetting?
Are we such incorrigible gold
that we just tarnish with time
awaiting polish to shine of old?
Or are we transmutable, by constant
additions of experience
toward a critical mass and change?

That's All

You always meant to smile
You know it and you kept it secret
The joy that came through others.
You saved and hid away
Until you were all alone
That moment no one saw
That no one even knew existed
That moment you saved
For a time to be renewed.
And, someday, when you're old
And all the colors turned with age
You'll remember all the moments
And think that's all that ever was—
The moments all were you.

Eidolon

Much whiter than the starlight on the snow
Your floating form beside me. Lighter flow
Your fluid movements than the dancing reams
Of particles from clouds where moonlights glow
And follow gliding patterns. And clearer seems
Each sparkling eye than any crystal streams
And in them truth that I might find and know
My lady made of dust from stars and dreams.

I wished, an instant, that you would be my lover
Though I knew that you would never love me
As a fleeting form that I could never hold
And I knew that I would rather not discover
That you are as free as the winds above me
And like the careless winds above me—cold.

Counting

I lay in bed on old stains of passion.
the world had stopped, events
everywhere tensed, massed.

How long did we love, how many times,
was each happiness more than before,
was it simply a matter of addition,
and we who measure our lives by numbers
must have a way to remember the past:
count our money, list our deeds,
accumulate some photographs to
display our lives—except the lives
were only preparations for the films,
diplomas, memories, to be looked back on,
finished, accomplished, separated, framed
and hung on the living room wall?

How else can I evaluate
the importance of our lives? Athletics,
rooms, and trophies, dances, dinners, and
poses, how does it look?
Struggles, reports, and stories, failure,
and comic-book love, how does it read?
First a car, then a place, one love, then
three—were any real?

Gone Away

Pretend I'm lost at sea,
Pretend I've gone to war,
Say I went off hunting
In wilderness unexplored—
It was involuntary.
It would be easier if it were true
So much easier if I had to go.

Yes, it would be better
If this was the last letter
From some tired suicide
Elegantly, quietly dying
Somewhere remote from you.
Pretend I'm sleeping
And leave me dreaming—

—dreaming in this chapel
Darkly wooded, dim aisles
Murmuring with sad prayers
For the wilted flowers
On the altar —
                    Love
That needs to go away
Needs, too, to return someday.

Probes

Probe I
Deeper it sinks—into nothingness
Groping here and around
Seeking all from inky blackness
Images faintly glow
Wan and wax
Intangible——free
Tresses of brown circling round
Warm breezes, span of green, whisper only,
"fair"———gone.

Probe II
Still on, endless infinity
And a silence only one born deaf knows
And a dark as one blind
A silver sun hurls
Motionless yet moving
Spinning forever
Clear blue skies, dancing eyes
Family and friends whisper only
"happiness"———gone

Prove III
Yet deeper where time is not
Ever searching
Black light stirs enmeshed in red
Bitter and burning, hating yet yearning
Both life and death whisper only
"war"———but no great armies, no weapons
impulses now dead whisper only
"nothing"
          what I see cannot be drawn
          what I feel cannot be expressed.

Slipping Underground

Seen through the light of cities at night
Shadows stately shadows tall
Obscure the filth in a black-grey pall.

Shadows no more to the blue-silver soar
Day light bright shows change but a face
Death abides in such a place.

A last beam of white flickers and dies
In darkness of black silence tells no lies
Danger, no need to be sought
With deadliness fraught is here.

Wind heralds end of night baring to all eyes and sight
Sea of green, ocean of night in warm currents giants grace
But death abides in such a place.

Anywhere and anytime dirt of town jungle of slime
In peace in violence
A look at the past vanished are all fears
Life is only worth so many years.

An agony of scream torn from the sound
A red crimson stream embraces the ground
Positions hard attained convulsions outraged
Senses remained.

Froth angry red with life of its own
From tortured lung spews from its own
To other colors imbues.

Eyes that see naught are eyes that are not
Covering with glaze, mind in a daze
Soul in a maze.

Life passes by routine way young to old wishing delay
Up to down, in to out, it comes tomorrow
It comes today.
Death unfeigned life unreigned.

Across the Sand

There was a land called Konicore
Above the heaven beyond the sun
And the people of this faraway land
Knew not war, knew not hun.

The purity of her cities
Gleaming distant silver white
Knew not decay, knew not age
Banned destruction, banned was blight.

Rules were few and far between
All to all were just and fair.
Greed and hate were never seen
A land of peace, tranquility there.

Generous people were these and kind
Good of soul with peace of mind
They needed no leader to guide their ways
Wealth filled coffers and planned were days.

In many other worlds things were quite bad
To think of all this made Konicore …
So all that they had they decided to share
To show the down-trodden they wanted to care.

A statue they carved of silver and gold
Upon it inscribed in characters bold
"Send me your sick, needy and poor,
Here there is happiness forevermore."

And people came from far away
How many there were no one could say
Not only the weak, not only the poor
But diseased, insane, criminal and more

Riots rebellion terror and crime
A world cried out, torn askew
The tranquility gone, gone for all time
What chance remained to start anew?

Yet, through all this Konicore grew
They turned to war to stem the tide
And before the sounds of battle died,
Countless were dead—all but a few.

Warmth was lost and hearts turned to stone
Rather than let their homeland decay
They fought for a decision among their own
And those who remained found a way.

A weapon made for total end
To every creature death to send
One instant the world was there
The next just black dust in thin air.

There is a land called Konicore
Above the heaven beyond the sun
And this solitary faraway land
Knows not war and knows not hun
Hot winds howl lonely across the sand.

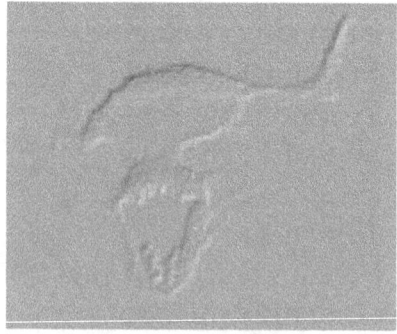

Ghost dolphin

Just as Blind

In silence he waits with patience
But his turmoil rages within
His own vivid fears his master's poison hates.

I walk with silence also alone, knowing fear
Sensing his presence near.
He thirsts, I know that too, with insatiable eyes
That glow in the night.
For I was told this was so.
As I walk, I wait for burning death, or slow.
What will it be like?
I pray for it not. Will I see him?
What will I do? When silence breaks
I stop. My terror awakes.

He sees the enemy standing there
An image reflecting in his shining dark eyes—
Would they dare to tell him lies? "Oh, masters,
Forgive, I cannot kill!" —quietly he turns and dies
Agony in blood, explosions in death.

I see the enemy turning his back
I must go also, must get away
It is not for me to die this day.
I start to turn and the world spins
As I fall, my weapon coughs
And then it's dark—I lay for years
Before I wake. Jungle sounds sound around
As I gather my feet, my bones they ache
But I live. I gaze about, mind in a daze
What? What lies there? So young
And so dead. Yes, my enemy—
They told me I'd find
The cold, heartless devil with eyes
Just as blind.

Three Prisons

1. Eaten by a bamboo dragon
captured by teeth and claws
and thrust down the tube
to lie in humid darkness.
Bamboo walls and vines
iron stand with porcelain bowl
a dirt bed with rags
that scatter when I wake
exercise and clean
memorize the grains
repetition without end
all life entertains
changing guards changing
seasons, changing me

2. Another day and all night long
with no place to lie down
open to air and water at Paia Mill
waiting for the light sleeplessly
rain here travels sideways
from the ocean through the trees
through the ventilators in the men's
room door, bringing the coolness
of night under flat fluorescent
light, paper towels on tile
paper towels for covers scatter
when I wake, stretch out concrete
ache, check for roaches or false
dawn and try to sleep again.
It's worth it for the sand and sun.

3. Pride and disappointment share
the patchwork bath and room
with a kitchen on the stairs.
Forty watts above my head
brings out the sculpture in old

plaster; dirt seems natural. I
finished trying to read and went
to bed, a single mattress dropped
between the stove and wall, warm
with all my clothes on. Ceiling rat patter
lullaby to sleep with no dreams.
Pigeons coo morning from the roof
and under peeling eaves. I watch
sunlight fill the corners through
cellophane stuffed broken glass
bathroom windows and make shadows
from ruined furniture—must escape Newark.

Three Wildernesses

1. I picked berries, knowing more would grow,
and went on, never looking back
to see if anyone followed,
but I knew they would,
in legions.
Green things growing wild, trails always new;
the trees cast shadows so long
it took a day to pass through.
Somewhere in the forest a vision came
stopped in sifted sunlight
spread his arms and
disappeared.
I dropped my kit by unnamed flowers
and lay on the cool moss:
this wilderness was mine
no one would enter here but I;
travelers looked, passing by
but kept on for their own
horizon.

2. I bought an apple at the grocery
for some change and moved back
into the crowds on the morning
sidewalk. asphalt streets in lines,
some trees in shadows
from buildings in the sun.
It took an hour of buses to reach home,
that uniquely numbered combination
of building blocks at intersections
and rooms on numbered floors.
I set my briefcase on the carpet
stretched out on an unmade bed
and looked at a wilted plant:
I thought this place a wilderness
and no one ever entered here;
people looked passing near, briefly,
from their hurriedness.

3. I thought of fresh fruit and wondered
where it grew or if I could get there.
I had come late to the earth,
after it had been stripped bare
from all the hungry years before.
What wonders held the ground
I did not know. I searched the clouds
of memory and found a wilderness
waiting: pieces from passages in books
and half-forgotten photographs; I gained
a vision of the mountain and tastes
from a hidden fountain: birds, trees,
scurrying sounds—all that I had hoped
for and expected—a separate virgin
planet with its own imaginary sun,
a cave, primeval well,
crystal life in its own cell:
This is the last wilderness
no one comes in or out, no one even cares
about the end of the wild universe.

The Fallen Garden

My life is uneventful—a sop
to promise, a symphony of innocence
until destroyed by the constant addition
of random noise: Eat, sleep,
drink, excrete, and then repeat.
Stand, futilely, as gravity draws us flat.
Storms allow no dignity, unanswered questions
leave no meaning; quantity is monotony;
occasional light radiates away. There is no heroism
in being full, no failure in emptiness, no honor
in duty, no purpose in living, no—

The world is not dedicated to saving beauty,
Life is not preparation for death, the whole
is not made to last, the song not saved
for the end. The boredom of life, for moments,
is replaced by the intense suffering of being.
But what fine, ripe fruits are produced
in this sad fallen garden, all
the pain of our lives, unseen
beneath the skin fills to fruition
and bursts at death—wet seeds
flung in the air—

Knowing Why

I've learned a few things (not that many, though).
I know why the leaves fall in October and I know
why the gopher snake bites when you pick him up.
I know why water runs downhill and where it goes
and I know why an owl flies and the lichen grows.

The leaves fall because the maple protects
itself from the dark and cold, and a snake bites
because he doesn't know you or your intention.
Water seeks a resting place, a stable situation,
and the owl has to catch her food, and lichens
are trying to split every barren rock open.

But don't ask me why you left me—did you need
to protect yourself? Did you not know me? Did
you need a place to rest where I would not pester
you? Were you hungry or did you just need to
degrade me? I don't know. I really don't know why.

But, I do know that now I am more at home
with snakes and owls, squirrels and lizards
than I ever will be with your ambitious
neglect. I know why a coyote howls, but not
why I must learn to. I know why a lion hunts
and rests alone, but not why I continue
to. I don't know why some swans don't mate for life
while others do. I don't know why some wolves
never mate and others do. I know why I want you
for life, but I don't know what you want—
I don't know and I know you can't tell me—
and I worry that it's too late, but I don't know why.

Alone in a World of Wounds

We murder in ignorance or by accident,
A thousand ways in a thousand moments—
Every footprint leaving bodies behind.

We kill for food or for convenience—
All living creatures feed on living;
Every hunger writes an autobiography
Of death. Our reverence is only
Acknowledgment of its necessity
And the fear of its consequences for us.

Our consciousness leads us from the whole;
That is how we know—in parts;
And that is its penalty. We must learn
Respect for iron, weeds, and flies
And grasp our way back.

Our obligation is to allow everything
That can to exist, not to control, promote
Or extinguish, but let each thing reach
Its full development.

Our duty is to feel, not transform or save,
To live, not evolve or finish, to respect
That the whole may feel in its diversity.

Our destiny is to turn the wheels
Of mortality and be turned under
Ourselves, that the earth may turn.

The Nexus of Permanence

This moment no one sees
this moment only me—
if all my past were resurrected
if my mind dissected
if all those moments could be counted
and carefully amounted
the moments would be almost all of me—
is all my life not these?

When my eyes could not discern things
the walls and furnishings
recorded all that could be heard and seen
in the deep vibrations in their being.

The most magical moments passed unnoticed
unnoticed by anyone else
unappreciated, they were scattered
as sound as light in matter
in waves to the trees, rocks and stars
into walls and floors
recorded by the earth in murmurings.

I give myself to my surroundings
all the weight of life
all that came before, became me,
and I will pass so easily.

Accomplishments

No one will make your house a monument
or put a marker at your place of birth;
there will be no great songs of fame—
no public recognition of your name.

What have your children ever done?
They never guided anyone by force
never tried to change or coerce
and they would always be hurt
rather than give pain in return.
They never piled up symbols,
and never tried living alone
for Art or God or Man—how
would they ever be known?
They never advertised themselves
or sold their way for money,
they worked no miracles, pushed
no claims to sainthood, just offered
kindness unnoticed, gentleness
unrecorded—and no importance
is paid to lives lived in balance
as well as they could be lived.

But this is enough for you, that
your all of children were good
that they gave and received help
to make the world a little better.

The Importance of Being Slow

If you're fast, there's always someone faster
but if you're slow, it really doesn't matter.
If you're fast, there's always someone to beat
but we who are slow have no reason to compete.

Being slow means that everyone can catch up
and nothing really passes by unnoticed.
There is nothing that cannot be grasped
eventually; nothing escapes slow attention.

Slowness adds another whole dimension
offering time to see what waits to be seen
the large and small and connections between
the lamp-post and star, the worm in bark.

The Lessons of Anonymity

Fail at the expectations of others.
Do not do anything fast. Do not advertise
Yourself, or sell. Forget the importance
Of names; know individuals. Claim nothing—
Accomplish less.
Be useless. Be part
of everything else.

Be full.
Be whole and regard the flow
Of wind and water. Be wind and water
And flow. Sit quietly doing nothing.
Be yourself.

Conceal yourself in the open
And remain unknown. Leave nothing
For your children; have no children.
Leave no trace for history.
No one will know whether or not
you ever existed.

The Ecstasy of Weeds

Snapdragon, fleabane, ragweed, the most
productive of plants. The seeds—dandelion,
milkweed, thistle—drift in the wind
and settle, bombs set to explode when
the ground is disturbed—thief or pioneer—
they seize their opportunities. Each seed
is a finger of life, probing to where life
is not. In extremes of heat drought and light,
each grows and holds moisture, retards
the wind, casts a spot of shade, and finally
surrenders its substance to others. Each
changes its place a little, reproduces
and perishes and all things follow and
nothing in their basic description prepares
you to witness their ecstasy at living.

Diverse and fertile, weeds wait
Outside a profusion of possibility.
Lupine lies frozen for ten thousand years;
Thistles rest on fence rows and roadsides;
Chamomile waits to colonize vacant lots.
Our skill at gathering wild plants
And herbs is lost, and with
It the value of weeds—
Who knows that couchgrass heals?
We know nothing of them. Seeking
Leads into wildness: Bluebells,
Rose, spiral racemes.
Where shall my soul dwell?
In immortal tansy.
And where is my home?
On earth in morning glory.

Lightbearer

I absorb light
from the sun during the day
or at least make it internal
so it can carry taste
and sound—at night
release it so I can see during the rare
times I can shed the verbal embrace
and try not to think or to speak.
I can still see, but the pulse of blood
quiets and slows
then I am dark
not as a shadow
or the absence of light
but dark as the space
where light has never reached
at the edge of being
or in my heart.

Darkness Still

I love the darkness
and it loves me, I believe—
not the darkness of the earth's shadow,
but where light has never been,
in my heart, in my brain, between stars,
where galaxies have yet to go, in the emptiness
before anything was —

The Dreams

World's End

Through rusted evening shadows to the edge of world's end,
I ran with wild abandon, ran with mad release.
I ran and ran across the coarse and cutting rocks, I ran
And blindly ran, then fell—
I suffered resurrection from the sinking seas of sleep,
a shocking tide of conscious light dissolved my coral dream
and dashed me on the shore of life. I rested low in dull
surroundings, in dark and dismal shrouds,
a futile figure set aloft from common , moving crowds.
No window needed open on the waking world below
for me to see the dim grey forms that wandered there, forever
 caught in prison shadows cast by insubstantial clouds.
In innocence, unwarned and lone I ventured from my barren
womb and sought the love and hate and sympathy of
humankind. But love and hate are selfish feelings, kept by men
for kindred, friends, and then themselves, and were not shared
with me. No sympathy was given me. I fled, and found
an isolated cell, in which I wove a separate thread upon
an unused loom. On private thoughts and private dreams
I wove my secret pleasures, made my secret joys and thus
surrendered conscious life to fantasy. I left the weary
world of suffering to live in light imagining. I dreamed alone,
apart, unburdened by existence, free from earth-burn sorrows,
free from pains of flesh. Then slowly, surely, terror crept
from deep Recesses, sucked by weakness from a hidden flaw,
and made my dreams its dreadful haunt. I feared an end,
would not let them end, for even with its heavy hollows,
life in dreams was yet a lesser rack   awherenow
than that of those who lived awakened lives. I chose to hazard
death in dreams: I fell on razor rocks and drowned
in choking seas and though I die in fume-dark
air, I never wish to wake, to wake to live and breathe
on moving, crowded shores, and so I shut my tired eyes to life
once more and slept and found my floating dreams.

I lay suspended, hung in ropes of pain, in muted
motionlessness 'til the twisted fibers broke—
gulped a burning breath and cried, for through the aching haze
I saw the harbor held no further sunlit days; a darkness
threatened that regretting tears could never brighten,
hopeless sighs would never lighten. I turned and gazed
at empty seas and empty skies that wings and fins
no longer filled; companions of the day were cold
and unconsoling, death was by their side and death had chilled
their presence; they had all withdrawn. I knew the night
was coming and I saw no future dawn. I looked along
the single stretching ridge that led to World's End, along
the continental spine where footsteps hurried unremembered
over ragged rocks that feet would never course again.
I scanned the jagged tip, the trailing tail that pointed past
the ocean to the brightly burning sun, beyond the red-rimmed
world where sank the setting sun. If that star is secretly
a guiding torch that leads To immaterial lands, I'll follow
it below the wash of waves on my immortal quest, but if it's just
a dying fire, becoming coldest ash, I'll follow just the same
and stay for one eternal moment's rest. I tensed myself
and straightened—quiet strength Was there. I stood and last
surveyed the lands and oceans of my world, a world
that took its fashion from my soul. I gave a sovereign's glance,
a solitary glance, for this was mine, my life, reality—
I stared beneath the cliff and saw some bubbles bursting in
a billow's wake; I stared and wondered when mine
would break—then, with the sun's last ray, I leapt—
whirling, multi-colored whirling, deeply tunneled,
steeply funneled swirling, with darkness at the end.

A brightness cleansed Me, enveloping warmth revived me, then
reluctant eyes from blue-light mists awoke to azure skies.
Each crystal ray of morning light reflected off ensorcelled seas
became my eye's own joy. I gasped a thrilling breath and floated
for a while in peace, then pulled by warm currents, pushed
by gentle waves, I gained the white-washed sands. I lay
and let my blood flow in throbs. I walked on wide-laid
grasses up the slope of glinting rocks. I swayed
before the breeze's soft insistent press, along the single
stretching ridge that marked the world's beginning—I woke.

The River of Return

I and my brothers went exploring
down a running hidden river
in a distant unnamed land. Where
it slowed by grasses
they went swimming in clear water
fighting mock fights with fishes,
but I held back, cautious, afraid,
disturbed by something, strayed
past rows and rows of shy trees peeked
between their trailing leaves—
found wooden boxes and metal crates
treasure left by someone long ago
packed to keep safe until—
I opened one, circumspectly
finding only strange familiarity—
it was mine, mine! All I'd ever owned
all that I had ever bought or sold,
all that I had lost or given away,
everything was here, packed away
in cartons that opened on command.
I called my brothers and they came
to help me count the things I had again
after so many careless years—
my books, , some still unread,
and clothes, all my clothes, records,
and lamps—we could not leave
them here now so we started
to load them in the boat.
Everything would be all right—
but we never did get out
everything vanished in the night
everything vanished in the day.

Not a Passenger

I drifted in the wind
                    and rested in white clouds
And then the wind would come
                            and tear my bed
And cover it with shrouds
                    then I would see
                    and I would know
That cloud would be my chariot
The running wind a horse
And I would be the only passenger
                            and where we'd go
                            I could not share
                            and when we'd stop
                            I would not care.

I rested on the ocean
                    and slept upon the swell
But the waves would roll
                    and turn my head
And try to smother me
                    and I would look
                    and understand
A wave would be my funeral barge
The stroking wind the oars
And I the only passenger
                    Beyond all land
                    And fellow men
                    This barge must float
                    Past time and then—

I drifted past the world's edge
                            past the harsh
And staring sun
                    through current-blackened space
To a cold and empty place
                    No wind or thought to stir
                    My vision starts to blur
This place is only emptiness
And I am not a passenger
                    No, I am not a passenger.

Core

The sky was red
The woods and distant plains around were wed
    By delicately woven airs
So very thin my passing shadow broke
Their gentle strains.

The sun had set
And each uncertain ray remaining met
    Uncertain shade of grey
And faded away as darkness spread
In purple strains.

The net of light
That burned so brightly
    Then evanesced as the world turned
Was made of day that left no ashes but
The black of night.

The current cut
I sank through shadows disconnected—
    Touched a branch, the ground
And found
The strength to whisper:
    There is a warmth within me
    That no cold dark can ever touch.

I laughed and dropped my hands
In dreams of perfect freedom
There were no passing shadows in this solid core
    The press of weight was gone
And no transparent chains
Restrained me anymore—
    left like a floating vessel
held at sea, least it reach a shore—
I stopped, in fear—

A sudden crack
In hidden clouds divided up the black
        And let the blades
From distant starpoints carve out figures
From the void.

A million strands
Of moonlight tied the trees to rolling lands
        But left my common bonds
With everything destroyed
And then I knew:
        There is a depth of coldness in me
        Where no warm sun will ever reach.

Dream Death

For the softest flowers that offer petals
for the breeze are anchored in the dirt
and I am like a summer blossom, my life
is but a blossom waving in air, that fades
and falls to the ground without its winds
and when the winds retire then a lighter
film of dust will lie upon the earth.
For the loveliest clouds that sail the skies
exist as only shadows on the earth
and I am like a cloud, my waking life
is just a shadow passing over, flowing fast
and disappearing when the sun has set
and after sunlight dies, then a deeper shade
of dark will dwell within the night.

War Dream

Normal until I reached the age of eighteen
I was taken—society demanded conformation,
Duty inescapable.
Pulled from all I knew so well
To some foreign-speaking country,
My mind balked. I slept.
Famous figures gathered round
Discussing great events to come,
And I was their leader—this was my world.
Uncounted millions and a food for every hunger,
Satisfaction for every craving, and I was rich—
        This was my world.
Sleek in every line, immense power,
beauty to dazzle, and I was her driver—
        this was my world.
Screaming thousands, strains of sound. Glory
And adoration. And I was their ruler—
        This was my world.
She most wonderful woman ever created,
And I was her lover—this was my world.
High in the heavens gold and silver clouds
And I was God.
        This also was my world.
A dank dark stillness, cold, and yet
Hot and foul. And I was dead—
        And this was my world.
Then it was time to wake
But always to a dank, dark stillness
Cold and yet hot and foul.
And I am dead.
        So, this is my world:
            Hell.

Did I Not Do That Too?

What did he really do? Just went
someplace before anyone else.
Of whom the statue? He was allowed
to rule over men. Of whom the painting?
She wrote unwritten thoughts—
And him and her? The others?
They arranged colors in pretty patterns
adding more elements of noise
to form as they got older.
Then he found chemical combinations
that helped others to live better.
She administered to the sick
while slowly wasting away herself.
He invented instruments to see differently,
He made a means of moving faster,
She acted out her fantasies for others,
And they moved in groves of swaying limbs.

Did I not do these things, not
discover unseen places, not change
things with my presence,
not see the world was petty
as well as sometimes spring and pretty?
Did I not?

I fell with the leaves in fall,
I knew, I chose,
I died and rotted and rose
as worms and grass and dew,
as birds I flew
as rivers I ran and flowed
in trees I stood again;
through paper, waves, and pen
I spoke
and still, I live in you
whole.

Monster of Night (Dream of the Dead)

He died in dirt, as a seed dies
transformed into a tree.

He tore loose his roots
and shook off leaves and bark
to free his limbs—
he walked again.

The sun dimmed
and sky solidified as ice
but nothing like
the weight of trees.

I saw him in the distance
fighting off silence,
he loomed gigantic;
the dead are strong—
he tore of pieces of the sky
to crush the town.

He roamed in twilight
over sinking ruins
seeking me.

He pinned me under a collapsed
house, pushed through stone
and rubble, reached through
timbers and pounded windows—
my lungs burned from powdered glass.

I drank from a dark puddle
rubbed my torn shirt
and shivered at the chill of moss.

He stood up, I called
but he did not answer. I heard
the road laid by his steps
and followed—
he never looked around.

Metamorphosis

Leaves grow at angles from the stem
So that each collects the light.
Light falls slowly like the dust
That leaves collect; it is held
And its crust forms the mask we see.
The leaves are burned by day,
Their colors are stripped by layers.
The leaves are ambiguous in the wind
When the walnut tree is astonished
By a storm.
Connections to the stem
Are subtle and easily overwhelmed.
Thin dry pages that once transmuted
Sun to flesh lie folded like meanings.
The leaves die and fall in winter;
Walnuts turn from green to black.
The tree stands in the cold air
With nineteen walnuts perfect and still.
A beetle in the bark digs deeper;
The center is dead, frozen cells
Surrounding nothing—a walnut turns
With a gust; the stem parts; the sphere
Turning becomes invisible and visible
Again in low sunlight. The walnut hits
The ground and splits open—there
Is no inside, only the one side folded over.
The birds of emptiness take wing.

Three Nights in the Heart of the Earth

Beneath the melilotus and the bee trembling
Over it, in the bright archegonium
Of ideas, the mind impregnates the object.

The seed is lost under clay and rock.
We forget the now not present, once of such
Importance. What we watch disappear
Our children will not ever know, or miss
As we did not miss what our parents forgot.
All poorer in experience.

Centuries end like nights; all things vital
Wear away, until the core is exposed.
The world slips in and out of focus
To human eyes as they age. The seed begins
To germinate, using its inheritance.
It develops in its coat: the meristem
Divides, and the leaf primordia intends.
It sends its roots to rock, where light
Dwells between grains.

Road Kill

Driving on the highway 26 through the channeled
Scablands in central Washington, I see an injured
coyote by the roadside. I stop,
get out, grab him, and put him in the back
of the sunburned Buick station wagon. Mark's body
is in the back, recently exhumed, wrapped
in canvas. As I am driving, I try again to raise
Mark from the dead. Suddenly, surprisingly,
I do but he goes immediately into the body
of the coyote. He is confused
and agitated. He keeps jumping
over the seat to look at me. Then jumping
to the back cargo and shitting. I try to explain
to him that it's the best that I could do.
I wasn't sure if it would work,
After so long, so much flesh lost.
Finally, he sits in the front seat and tentatively licks
my hand. I stroke his head. It smells of wet fur
in the car. I open the window a little.
We drive down the road without headlights.
As we travel, I gather everything in,
but I am not enough to hold it—

Coyote Loves to Hide

Nature loves to hide
    and nature loves to play
                play at hiding
hide at playing
        display
show and turn and expect you to remember
        We remember even as we see again
and the present expands

Nature loves to hide and tease
                but coyotes love to seek
    humans love to seek and please
And so we seek each other and play
        And hide within nature
our nature her nature his nature
        all the natures that exist.

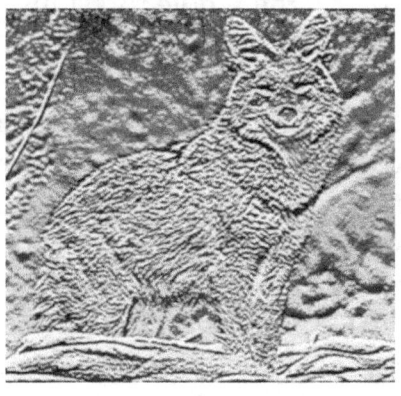

Forest Passage

I didn't tell anyone where I am, just like I didn't tell
anyone there where I was going. Now, I'm in the forest,
but I'm not alone, no, everyone here has heard me
stumble through the brush and vines, but they let
me go my own way. The painted turtle couldn't escape
and had to be held, as unwilling as you but easier
to catch. He showed me the direction to the stream.
The bull snake path pulled my gaze to the berries
that were old but very sweet. I poked into the old
dry leaves that crinkled with his passage—
never caught him, never saw him.

Fir trees protect me from the sun; a breeze winds around
me exhausted from forcing its way past the edge trees'
low boughs, but welcome and scented. A chipmunk
scrambles out of reach along a log, certain that I'm hungry
for her—and only her—flesh. Across the sky, the eidolons
flirt before turning into merely clouds. Birds sing and let
me know when someone's coming so I can hide as well.
Turkey buzzards patrol the whole forest just
above the treetops. I'm not upset, I'm not afraid;
the harm that's possible here is not the cruel kind. Bear
rambles along, leaving berry-rich piles of dung; I poke it
with a stick to see if it's still warm. It is. Now it's dark,
I walk through the trees just slightly darker than the deer
trail slightly darker than the sky beyond. A mountain lion
watches without giving away her position—I know
because I smell her, slightly stronger than the leaves.
Every passing moment something human slips away
from me like fog at night. I am incapable of feeling,
although I can move quietly like the lion through
the needle-dry trees. I am as cool as the moss that grows
over old logs. I am as dark as the soil under decayed
wood. I am as content as the black bear with the richness
of fall berries. Every day I close myself a little more
to useless information. Soon I will be incapable of speech.

Memories

Are memories not like leaves
piling up when trees are bare
blown about in winter loosely held
to earth, then rotting and decaying
as new ones start to form immediately,
decomposing to humus for nourishing
that same tree another season?

Are memories not like raindrops
condensing in the mists
of a too-oft tired mind, small impurities
adding layers falling through
the levels of a complicated cloud
growing in size, gathering a charge
precipitating with the weight of having?

Authors

The Band of Brothers never forgets, never rests, never lets one another be forgotten or be missed, even if we have to haunt your dreams—

The Editor

Morgan Hood Wolfe is a careless craftsman of word images. He was classically trained by his reading of famous old poets and by his attempts to duplicate their forms. He lost much of his knowledge in formal university training, and has been striving to recover it ever since, as well as to recover a little of the joy in spontaneous learning.

Colophon
This book is set in Palatino
Using Indesign
On a Macintosh Ibook
And composed on Coquina Beach
Paintings & Photographs by A.M. Caratheodory
Music & drinks by Precious Woulfe
Book and Cover design by Rian Garcia Calusa
Printing & assistance by Booksurge

www.ingramcontent.com/pod-product-compliance
Lightning Source LLC
Chambersburg PA
CBHW071207130626
46555CB00004B/1610